For Barry, Maisie & J.J.

Thanks to my amazing other half Barry Simpson, for without his keen eye for detail, my book would not be what it is. Thank you also to my Mum Margaret, Elaine Coburn, Irene Lunny-Blair, Maggie Miller, Jill McDaid and Katrina Bryan for all their help and support. Thanks also to Paul Brown & Michelle Fraser and Rab & Jan Moir.

Kitty Cat Publishing LTD, Summit House, 4-5 Mitchell Street, Edinburgh   EH6 7BD
www.kittycatpublishing.com

Published 2014
ISBN 978 0 9574326 3 5

Text and illustrations ©Catherine Muir 2013.
All rights reserved

D1439385

If you like this book, please visit

www.scarletunderpants.com

for more titles

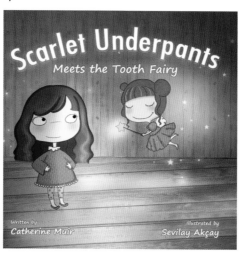

Scarlet Underpants
Meets the Tooth Fairy

Written by
Catherine Muir

Illustrated by
Sevilay Akçay

More titles coming soon

Look out for
"The Wheelie Wonderful Life of Millie Monroe"

by Kim Tserkezie

Scarlet Underpants

Meets the Dragon

Written by
Catherine Muir

Illustrated by
Sevilay Akçay

Scarlet lay in bed thinking about meeting the tooth fairy, Penny Moneytree and she wondered if it was all real.

She sighed as she dropped off into a lovely sleep.

Scarlet dreamed of fairies and dragons and chocolate and shoes all night long.

When she woke up, she wanted to eat chocolate and wear some sparkly shoes.

She laughed out loud as she thought, "I hope I don't get that the wrong way round!"

Scarlet does not **normally** get up until 10 minutes after she has to. But not today.

Today she was up, out of bed and in front of the treehouse very quickly.

"Hello, Penny?" Scarlet said as she wondered if it had all been a dream.

"It's not very **realistic** after all."

She said out loud, "I don't know what I was thinking, a fairy living in my treehouse. I must be nuts!"

Just then she heard a voice, "Don't say that too loudly or the squirrels will be down to see if there really are nuts."

It was Penny!

"Good morning Scarlet Underpants! Aren't you usually still in bed at this time?"

"I thought I dreamt you, along with the chocolate shoes and sparkly shoes the dragon had on," said Scarlet with a relieved tone to her voice.

"Chocolate shoes?
Those shoes would NOT be nice to eat if you wore them on your feet!

Scarlet, you will need to be here at 4.15 p.m. exactly today," said Penny. "Do not, whatever you do, be late. Dragons really do not like it when you are late!"

"Okay Penny, I'll see you at 4.15 p.m. today. Do I need to bring anything,

fire extinguisher or anything?"

"Don't be silly," said Penny. "Fire extinguisher indeed, but if you can, bring liquorice. Dragons love liquorice!"

Scarlet could not wait for school to finish, she was very excited and wanted to tell everyone about the tooth fairy and her friend, a real live dragon, coming to dinner today!
But she thought she better not, as no-one would probably believe her!

When the bell rang at the end of the day, Scarlet ran home as fast as she could.
She felt like there was smoke coming from her feet because she was running so fast.

When Scarlet arrived home, she went to the kitchen to find some liquorice.

She looked through the drawer full of sweet things and at the bottom was a bag of mixed liquorice. "I hope it's the mixed kind the dragon likes," she thought, since that was the only kind they had.

She wondered what to wear to meet a dragon….
As she tried on different clothes she looked out of the window at the treehouse.
Daddy worked very hard to build it and now a tooth fairy had it for her home! WOW!

Eventually it was 4.10 p.m.

Scarlet went downstairs and picked up the liquorice on her way out to the treehouse.

"Hello. Penny, it's me Scarlet." She said now a little nervous.
"Come in Scarlet Underpants, come and meet my friend, Rarajaja."
Scarlet looked around but could not see anything.
"Where is he?" Scarlet asked looking puzzled.

"He is right there, in front of you! Can't you see him?" Penny asked.

Scarlet looked down to where Penny was pointing, and down, way down was a tiny little dragon.

"Oh, I'm very sorry, I didn't see you there. I didn't expect you to be so tiny," Scarlet said.

Rarajaja started to cry. "Is she making fun of me for being small? That's not nice!" said the dragon.

"What?" said Scarlet, a bit **surprised** to say the least.

"Why is Rarajaja crying?" Scarlet asked, very confused now. "I thought they were big scary, fire breathing monsters?" she said.

Rarajaja cried some more.

"The mean elves made up stories about us," the dragon wailed.
"Scarlet Underpants!" said Penny. "I explained that yesterday. Dragons are really sensitive!"

"I'm very sorry for upsetting you." She said.

Rarajaja stopped crying and explained, "Dragons are just a little

sensitive from time to time."

"I'm like that too sometimes," said Scarlet. "Mummy is always saying to me not to get upset when the other kids tease me.

Why did the elves make up stories about you?"

Rarajaja didn't answer but started to sniff loudly, "Is that liquorice I smell?"

Scarlet smiled and handed the liquorice to Rarajaja. "Thank you," he said.

Penny smiled at Scarlet, then turned to Rarajaja, "Don't eat too much because dinner is almost ready."

"Come and sit," said Penny as she **ushered** everyone to the table.

She started to serve lots of strange coloured, shaped foods.

"What is this?" asked Scarlet.

"It's fairy food," Penny said.
"Eat up now, it's very good for you," she added.
Scarlet lifted up a little of the food on her plate and thought she better eat it and not offend Penny.

She put it in her mouth and her mouth started to **tingle**.

Her throat started to tingle, her tummy started to tingle.

Scarlet started to laugh and with this laugh, she started to float.

Rarajaja looked at Penny. "Has she never had fairy food before?" he asked.
"No, I don't think so," answered the fairy.

She looked round at Scarlet who was now flat against the ceiling of the treehouse laughing her socks off.
"Scarlet, take my hand and let's go for a fly," said Penny.

As Scarlet took Penny's hand, she realised, now they were all the same size.

"What's happened to me?"

Scarlet was still laughing as she asked this question.

"You are tiny so we can have a fly. It would not look very good if you were flying around at your normal size, now would it?" Penny answered.

"Will I be like this forever?" asked Scarlet, while thinking, "no wonder the dragon was crying when I thought he was small. I wonder if this is what happened to him?"

She didn't want to ask now in case he started crying again.

Now she was this small, she might drown in his tears.

Penny smiled at Scarlet as she started to fly out of the door of the treehouse. Scarlet and the dragon followed behind her.

Scarlet was really scared at first but once they flew above the trees and the birds and the clouds, it was the most

wonderful feeling ever!

She felt so peaceful.

Scarlet also felt so light and special.

Really, really, special.

Just then Scarlet's tummy **rumbled**.

They started falling downwards.
Scarlet shouted as loud as she could, "What's happening?"

They were falling faster and faster.
Scarlet looked down at her hand and it was getting bigger!

She looked at the tooth fairy and realised her fairy food must be wearing off now.

The tooth fairy was trying to get them back as quickly as possible. Scarlet was getting bigger and they were falling even faster now. Faster and faster and faster!

Just at that Scarlet thought she could see her treehouse, her back garden

and her trampoline.

She knew what Penny was going to do. She was aiming to drop Scarlet on the trampoline.

Penny let Scarlet go and she dropped down onto the trampoline.

Scarlet felt very dizzy and very wobbly too. She went over to the treehouse and shouted in a

whisper,

"Penny, Penny are you there?"

Scarlet climbed into the treehouse and heard Penny say, "See what happens when you don't eat all your dinner?"

Scarlet thanked her friends for a wonderful experience.
She thought to herself, tomorrow she would talk to Penny about having a word with the king of the elves. Perhaps the elf king would apologise to Rarajaja for making up stories.

"Making up untrue things about people is awful," Scarlet thought to herself.

"Scarlet, great timing," said Mum. "Go and wash up for dinner please."
Scarlet nodded and then asked, "Where is J.J.?"

Her Mother laughed and pointed under the table.

When J.J. saw Scarlet, he stuck out his head and said, "Boo!"
She smiled at him and went to give him a hug. J.J. saw what Scarlet was
going to do and disappeared under the table as fast as he could. She
shrugged her shoulders and thought about what a great day she had flying
with a tooth fairy and a dragon.

WOW!

Scarlet felt she was the luckiest girl in the whole world.

The Luckiest Girl

In The Whole World

Catherine Muir is a dedicated Mum of two who has worked in children's television for many years.

Having taken some time out to spend with her children, she found some interesting ways to entertain them.

This book is based on a character that developed over the years of nursing illnesses, dealing with the everyday problems of growing up and telling stories when kids sometimes need a little subtle guidance.

www.scarletunderpants.com

If you like this book, please visit

www.kittycatpublishing.com

for more titles

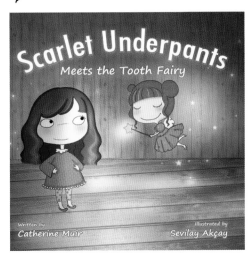

More titles coming soon

Look out for
"The Wheelie Wonderful Life of Millie Monroe"

by Kim Tserkezie